INVERCLYDE LIBRARIES

CW00260038

Courageous Lucy

For Lucinda, who wanted a book
and Sue, who deserves a library.
— P.R.

For Mum and Dad. Thank you for
your constant love and support.
— C.K.

First published 2021

EK Books
an imprint of Exisle Publishing Pty Ltd
PO Box 864, Chatswood, NSW 2057, Australia
226 High Street, Dunedin, 9016, New Zealand
www.ekbooks.org

A CiP record for this book is available from the National Library
of Australia.

ISBN 978-1-925820-77-5

Designed by Mark Thacker
Typeset in Minya Nouvelle 18 on 26pt

Printed in China
This book uses paper sourced under ISO 14001 guidelines
from well-managed forests and other controlled sources.

10 9 8 7 6 5 4 3 2 1

Courageous Lucy

The girl who liked to worry

PAUL RUSSELL & CARA KING

Lucy worried about **everything.**

Lucy worried about normal things, but often she worried about things that other people didn't even know to worry about. Lucy worried that one day her shadow might turn into a giant black hole and swallow her up, or that she might accidentally run into the end of a rainbow.

Lucy worried that she might be the first one to
discover Bigfoot on the same day he stubbed his toe ...

or that she might meet the Queen of England
on the way to school, but forget her name.

In short, Lucy worried about everything and she worried a lot.

Lucy didn't like going first because
she didn't want to make a mistake.
But she didn't like going last because
she was worried she would miss out.

Lucy knew lots of things.
Lucy knew why stars
twinkle. She knew why
water appears blue.

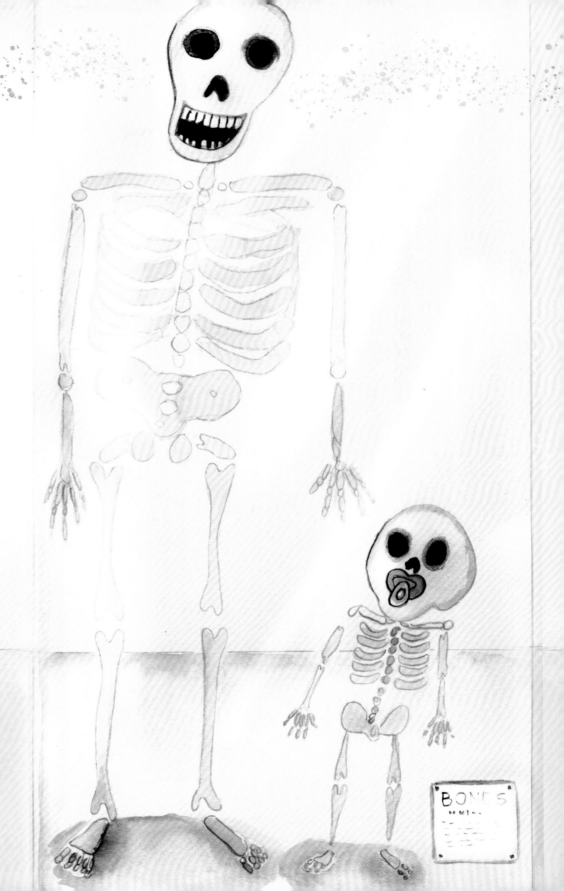

She knew the capital of Brazil and why humans have 270 bones when they are born but only 206 as adults.

But Lucy was too worried to tell anyone what she knew.

When Mrs Hunt put up a poster for the
school musical, the class was excited.

Lucy wasn't.

She worried that there might be too many people in the audience or they could get stuck in the hall and the stage might collapse.

When Mrs Hunt started auditions, Charlie sang a song about rainbows and Henry sang a song about chocolate cake.

Georgia did a dance for her audition and Andrew had a full pirate costume.

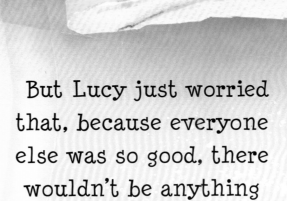

But Lucy just worried that, because everyone else was so good, there wouldn't be anything left for her.

Max brought in his recorder and Jordan's dad made a giant box to stand on.

When Mrs Hunt asked for help, Eve brought in costume designs and Ryan found an old black shirt so he could help backstage.

But Lucy didn't know how
she could help, even though
she really wanted to.

'Mrs Hunt, I would like
to be in the musical,'
Lucy said after finding some
bravery she didn't know she had.

'Can you sing, Lucy?'

Mrs Hunt asked with a kind smile, but Lucy shook her head.

'Can you be courageous?'

Mrs Hunt said. Lucy thought for a moment and although she wasn't *sure* she could, she thought she *might*, so she nodded and Mrs Hunt handed Lucy a script.

SCHOOL
MUSICAL

AUDITIONS
THIS WEEK

It was for the part of the tree. The tree didn't have any lines but Mrs Hunt told her it was a very important part, as she would be on stage the entire time. And, in the woodcutter scene, Lucy had to fall over.

CPSIA information can be obtained
at www.ICGtesting.com
Printed in the USA
BVRC100805230821
615013BV00008B/274

Lucy practised swaying in the
imaginary wind while Charlie
sang songs about new beginnings.

Lucy practised dropping her
leaves when Andrew sang about
dragons and castles.

When everyone practised
their bows, Lucy practised
falling over.

When the big night came, Lucy stood up on the stage, and although her knees were knocking and her tummy was tied up in knots, she was the best tree anyone could ever remember. Everyone said it was the greatest performance the school had ever done.

Lucy still worries that there might be an earthquake that causes the entire school to vanish, or Aliens could choose her to travel to distant planets without her parents, but ...

... even though Lucy still
worries, she also knows
that sometimes you can be
courageous too.